HORSE & BUGGY

DANCE, DANCE, DANCE!

I Like to Read® books, created by award-winning
picture book artists as well as talented newcomers,
instill confidence and the joy of reading in new readers.

We want to hear every new reader say, "I like to read!"

HORSE & BUGGY
DANCE, DANCE, DANCE!

Ethan Long

I Like to Read®

HOLIDAY HOUSE • NEW YORK

What are you doing?

I am dancing.

I am the best dancer.

I have the best dances!

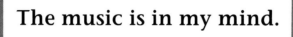

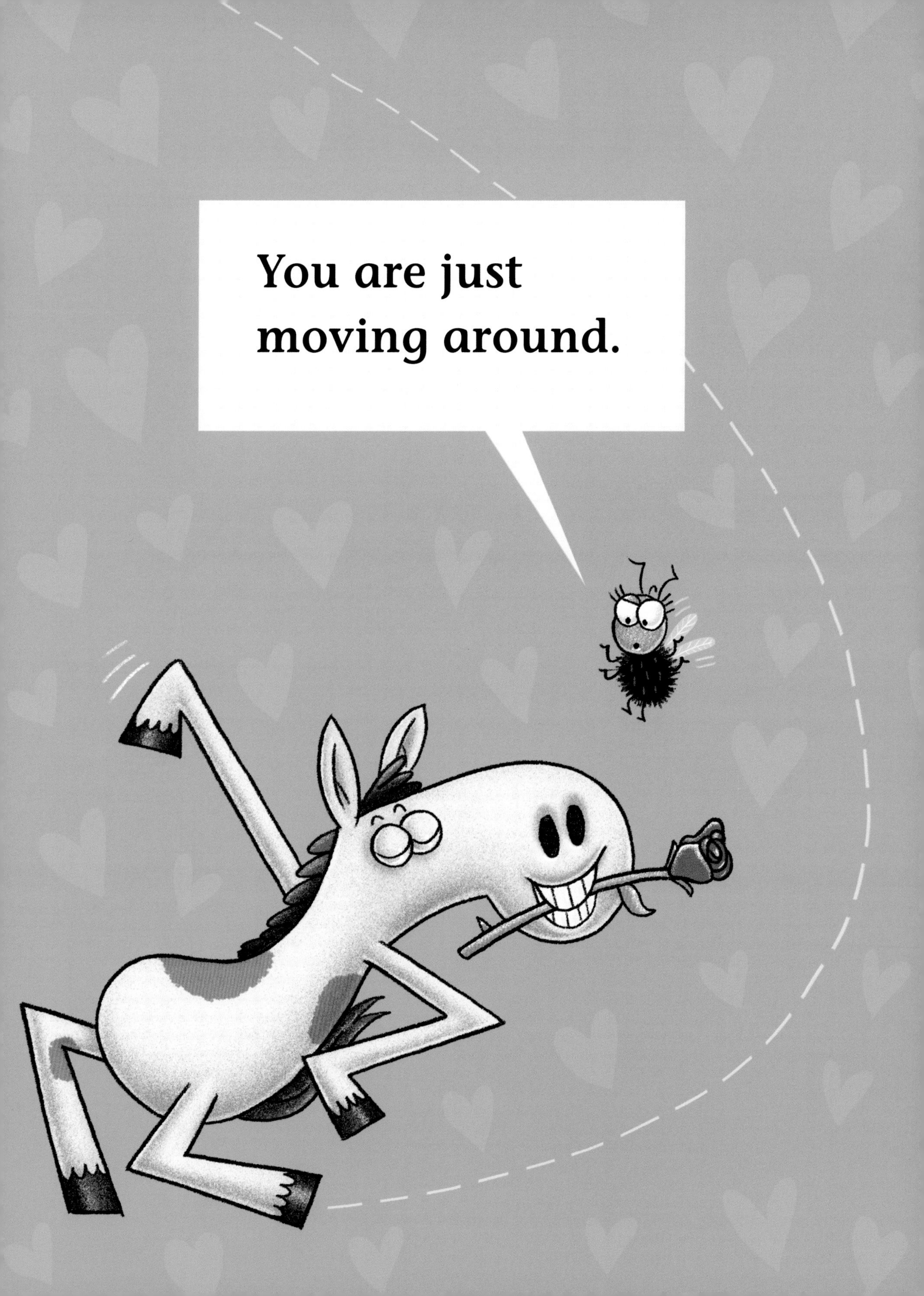
You are just moving around.

And now you look like a robot.

This dance is called the robot!

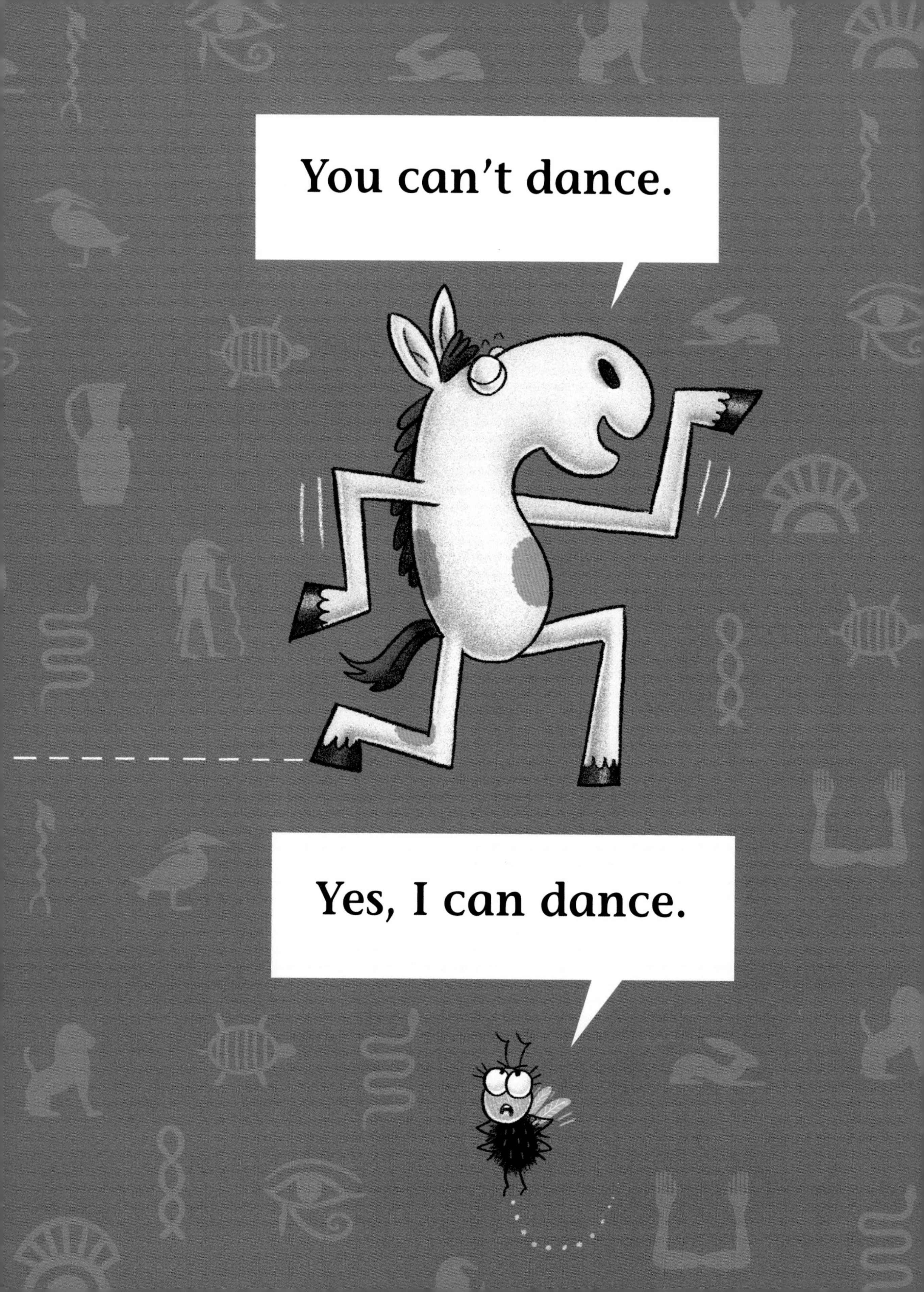
You can't dance.
Yes, I can dance.

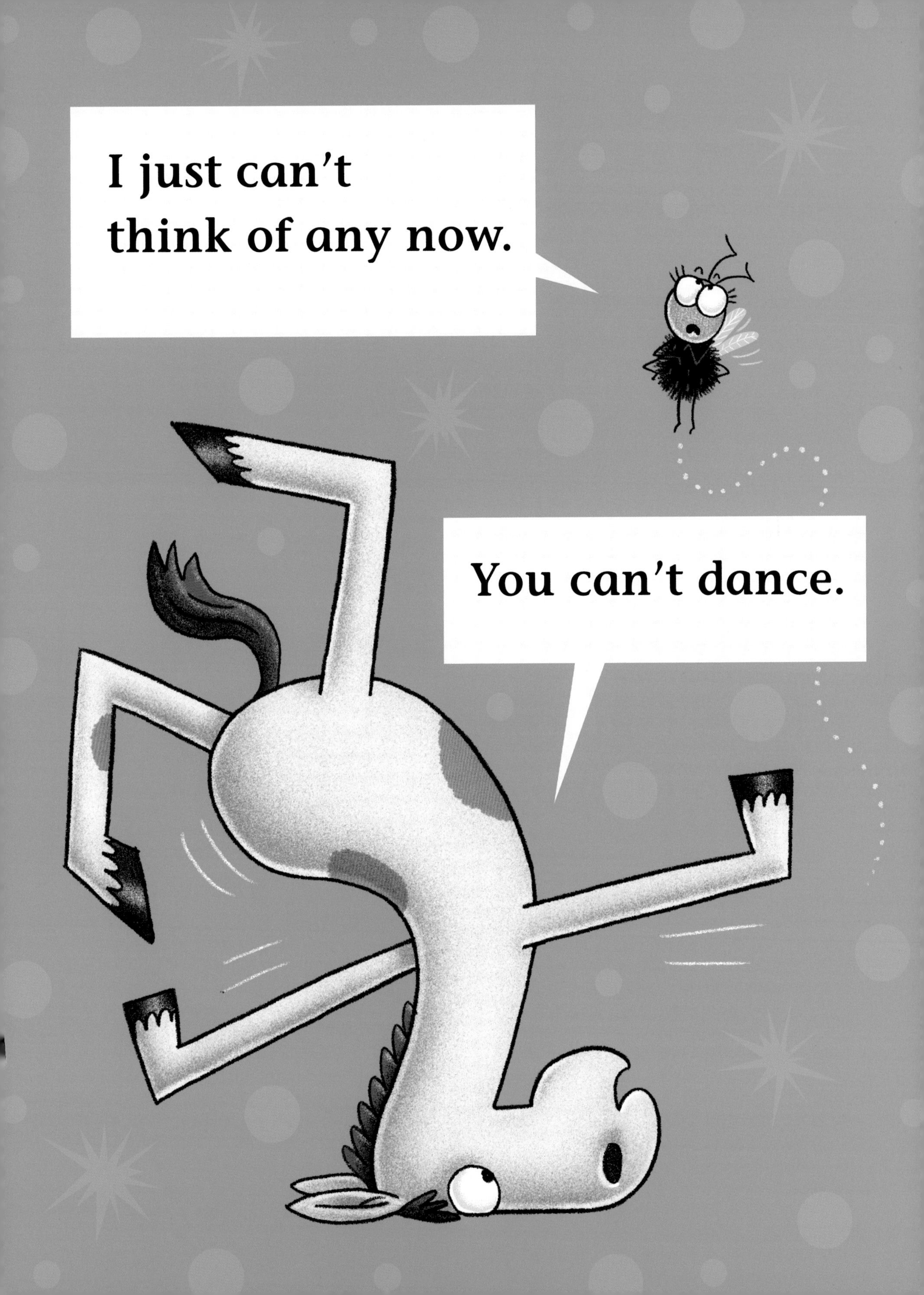
I just can't think of any now.
You can't dance.

There. I danced.
Are you happy now?

I am not happy.

Because you are not happy.

So turn off the frown.
Start getting down!

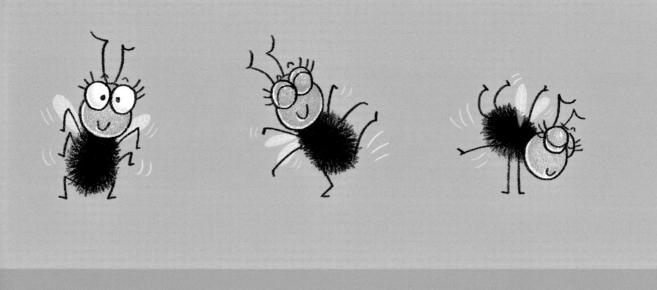

Horse?

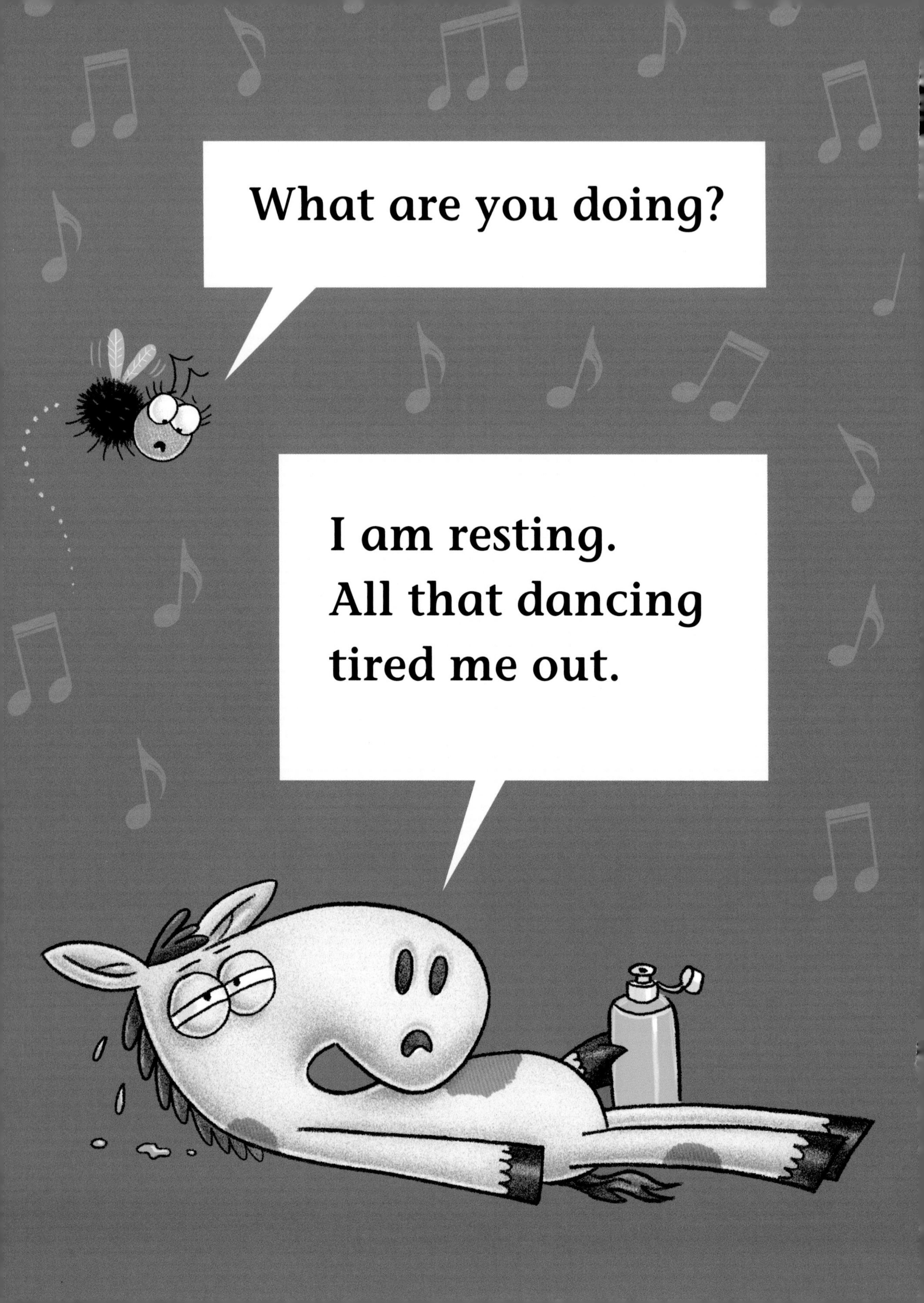
What are you doing?
I am resting.
All that dancing
tired me out.

I LIKE TO READ is a registered trademark of Holiday House Publishing, Inc.

Copyright © 2018 by Ethan Long

HOLIDAY HOUSE is registered in the U.S. Patent and Trademark Office.

Printed and Bound in November 2017 at Tien Wah Press, Johor Bahru, Johor, Malaysia.

The artwork was created digitally.

www.holidayhouse.com

First Edition

1 3 5 7 9 10 8 6 4 2

Library of Congress Cataloging-in-Publication Data is available.

ISBN 978-0-8234-3859-4 (hardcover)

ISBN 978-0-8234-3968-3 (paperback)

Check out these other I Like to Read® Level E readers!

Visit www.holidayhouse.com/ILiketoRead

for more about I Like to Read® books, including flash cards, reproducibles,

and the complete list of titles.